FERGUS

Based on *The Railway Series* by the Rev. W. Awdry

Illustrations by
Robin Davies and Jerry Smith

EGMONT

EGMONT

We bring stories to life

First published in Great Britain in 2006
by Egmont UK Limited
239 Kensington High Street, London W8 6SA
All Rights Reserved

Thomas the Tank Engine & Friends™

A BRITT ALLCROFT COMPANY PRODUCTION

Based on The Railway Series by The Reverend W Awdry
© 2007 Gullane (Thomas) LLC. A HIT Entertainment Company

Thomas the Tank Engine & Friends and Thomas & Friends are trademarks of Gullane (Thomas) Limited.
Thomas the Tank Engine & Friends and Design is Reg. US. Pat. & Tm. Off.

HiT entertainment

ISBN 978 1 4052 2653 0
3 5 7 9 10 8 6 4
Printed in Great Britain

*T*his is the story of Fergus, a little traction engine who always liked to "do things right". One day, I asked him to help Bill and Ben at the Quarry, but poor Fergus wasn't used to their tricks. Read about the trouble they caused him . . .

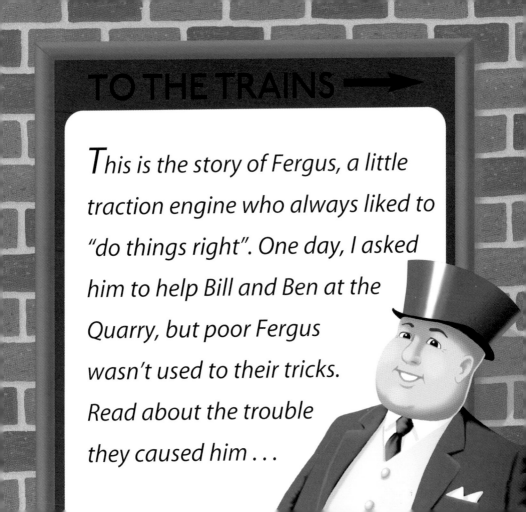

Fergus the little blue traction engine was the pride of the Cement Works.

He loved his work. He knew all the rules and always stuck to them.

One morning, he was chuffing cheerfully across the Island of Sodor. He was on his way to do a special job for The Fat Controller.

As Fergus reached the station, there stood Thomas. He was waiting for his passengers to board Annie and Clarabel.

Thomas gave a friendly "Peep! Peep!" on his whistle. "Hello, Fergus!" he said.

"I'm off to work in the Quarry today," Fergus told Thomas, proudly.

"Watch out for Bill and Ben," Thomas warned. "They like to get up to mischief!"

"Thank you, Thomas. I won't let a couple of rascals get the better of me," wheeshed Fergus.

When Fergus arrived at the Quarry, Mavis and the twins were waiting for him.

Mavis was pleased that Fergus had come to help, and they set to work straight away.

"I'm afraid the trucks are in a mess," she said.

"Not to worry," puffed Fergus kindly. "We'll soon sort them out together."

Bill and Ben grinned with delight.

"Now we'll have some fun!" whispered Ben.

"We'll have the old boiler in a spin!" steamed Bill.

Fergus was happy working with Mavis. "She is a Useful Engine, just like me," he thought to himself.

But Bill and Ben were not behaving like Useful Engines at all. Bill banged his trucks so hard that some rocks fell out on to the track.

"Steady!" called Fergus. "Do it right!"

"I know what I'm doing," wheeshed Bill.

Then Ben left his trucks on the points so that Fergus couldn't get out of the siding.

"You've boxed me in," steamed Fergus. "Shift those trucks out of my way. Do it right!"

But Ben just grinned.

The next day, the works crew was blasting rock. The siren sounded to tell the engines that there was danger ahead. There was a loud "BOOM!" and a cloud of dust filled the air.

"Wait for the all-clear, listen for the siren," Fergus told Bill and Ben. "Do it right!"

"There he goes again!" said Bill. "'Do it right', 'do it right'. It's all he tells us, from morning until night!"

"Keep your big funnel out of our Quarry!" huffed Ben rudely.

Later, the Quarrymaster sent Bill and Ben to collect a new rock crusher from the Harbour.

Fergus spent a happy afternoon shunting trucks with Mavis.

The Quarry was a much more peaceful place without the twins around!

At the Harbour, Bill and Ben were still cross with Fergus.

"He's always telling us what to do," moaned Bill.

"He always says 'Do it right!'" said Ben.

"Next time he tells us what do . . ." wheeshed Bill.

"We'll do it wrong!" Ben said.

With the rock crusher safely loaded on to a flat truck, Bill and Ben steamed back to the Quarry as quickly as they could.

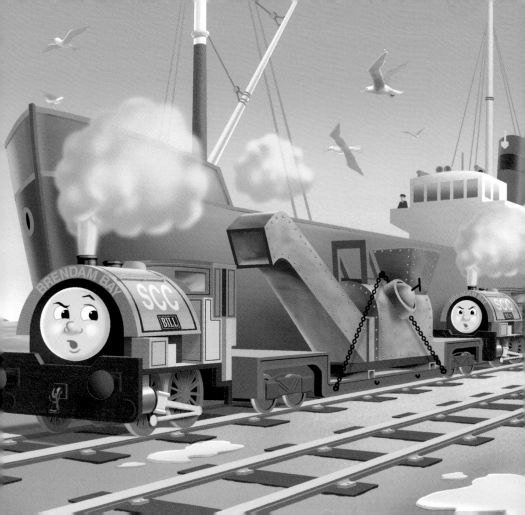

The rock crusher was heavy. It made the rails shake all the way back.

Fergus was waiting for Bill and Ben to arrive. "The blasting has made the rock face unsafe," he called to them. "Stay away! Do things right!"

Bill and Ben didn't listen. They rattled their load towards the cliff as roughly as they could.

Suddenly, loose rocks and stones began to fall from the rock face.

"Look out!" wheeshed Fergus.

"Help!" wailed Bill and Ben together.

Fergus steamed forward and banged Bill and Ben out of the way. His Driver jumped clear just in time but the falling rocks buried Fergus, right up to his funnel.

Mavis and the twin engines worked busily to carry away the rocks and rubble.

It took a long time to dig poor Fergus out. No one worked harder than Bill and Ben to try and rescue the little traction engine.

They didn't moan and there were no tricks.

They wanted to do things right.

At last, Fergus was free.

Bill and Ben were very ashamed of themselves. "We shouldn't have been so naughty," said Bill.

"We're very sorry, Fergus!" added Ben.

"As long as we're friends again now," smiled Fergus.

"Oh, yes!" said the twins together.

"Good," smiled Fergus. "From now on, we'll do things right together."

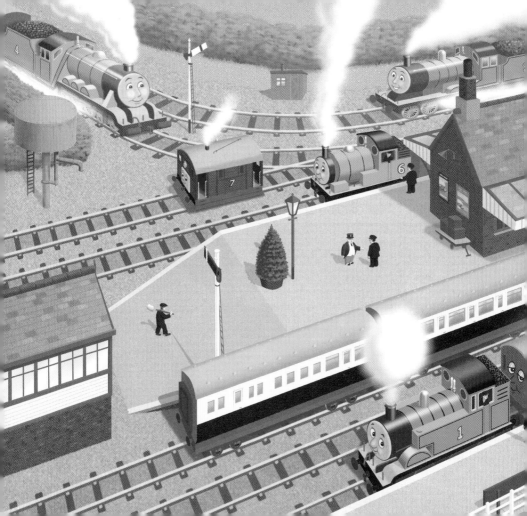

The Thomas Story Library is THE definitive collection of stories about Thomas and ALL his Friends.

5 more Thomas Story Library titles will be chuffing into your local bookshop in April 2007:

Arthur

Caroline

Murdoch

Neville

Freddie

And there are even more
Thomas Story Library books to follow later!

So go on, start your Thomas Story Library NOW!

A Fantastic Offer for Thomas the Tank Engine Fans!

STICK POUND COIN HERE

In every Thomas Story Library book like this one, you will find a special token. Collect 6 Thomas tokens and we will send you a brilliant Thomas poster, and a double-sided bedroom door hanger! Simply tape a £1 coin in the space above, and fill out the form overleaf.

TO BE COMPLETED BY AN ADULT

To apply for this great offer, ask an adult to complete the coupon below and send it with a pound coin and 6 tokens, to:
THOMAS OFFERS, PO BOX 715, HORSHAM RH12 5WG

☐ Please send a Thomas poster and door hanger. I enclose 6 tokens plus a £1 coin. (Price includes P&P)

Fan's name...

Address..

....Postcode..........................

Date of birth..

Name of parent/guardian...

Signature of parent/guardian..

Please allow 28 days for delivery. Offer is only available while stocks last. We reserve the right to change the terms of this offer at any time and we offer a 14 day money back guarantee. This does not affect your statutory rights.

☐ Data Protection Act: If you do not wish to receive other similar offers from us or companies we recommend, please tick this box. Offers apply to UK only.